LINUS

STUART HAUSMANN

A
atheneum

Atheneum Books for Young Readers

New York London Toronto Sydney New Delhi

The citizens of Linneopolis were an uptight, straitlaced bunch.

They were punctual.
They were orderly.
And they drew the line
at anything that bent their
world out of shape. . . .

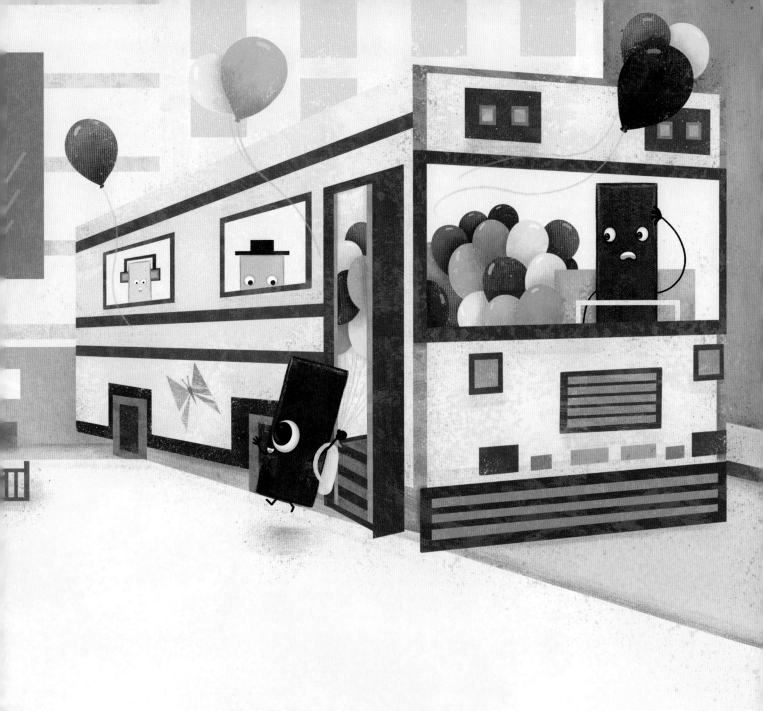

But not Linus.

Linus loved shapes.

Linus loved colors.

And Linus especially loved
finding a reason to celebrate.

"Linus, we come from a proper, upright lineage,"
the Line Leader explained.
"All of this acting up is way out of line!
Perhaps you could tone it down a bit?"

**But the more Linus
tried to toe the line,**

**the more bent out
of shape he became.**

We need to talk.

Linus followed the Line Leader
to the edge of town.

I'd like to introduce you
to the Builders Club.

I think this will be a perfect opportunity for you to build character, straighten back up, and return to being the Linus we know and love!

They build all sorts of neat things at their weekend retreats!

That night, as the others slept, Linus stood wide awake.

I need **colors.**   *I need* **shapes.**   *I need . . .*

to get away.

The farther Linus went . . .

the more things changed.

All eyes were on Linus
as he made his way into town.
The people of Squiggleville
were skeptical at first,

but they soon discovered
Linus made their world
a little more special.

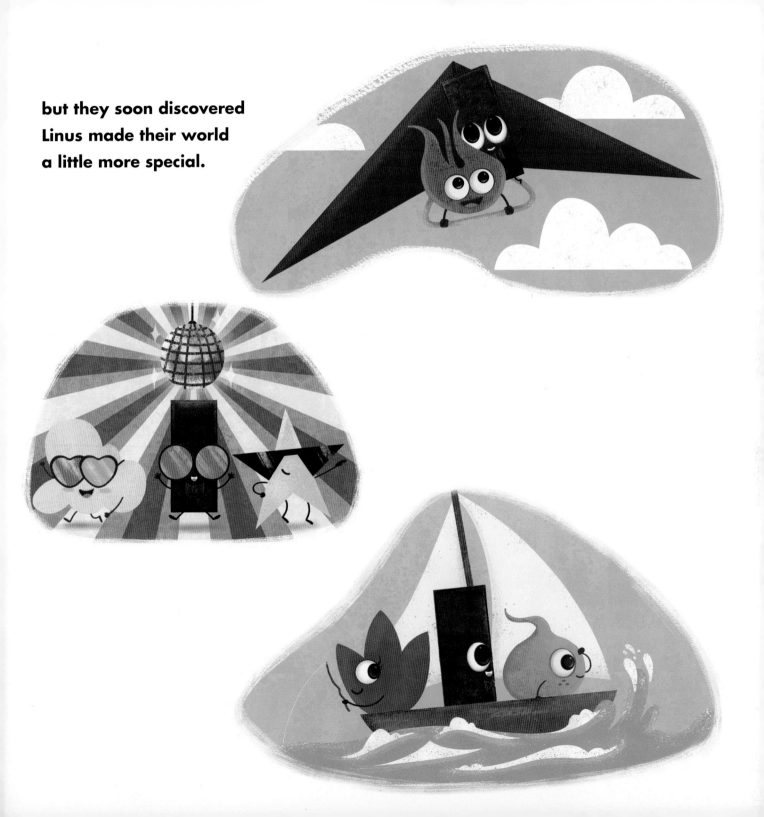

But to Linus's surprise,
he was starting to miss home.

*If only I could show my friends
there's nothing to fear!*
Linus thought.

*If only I could bring everyone together!
If only . . .*

Suddenly, Linus had an idea.

"Linus!" the Line Leader cried.
"We were worried sick about you!
Don't you know it's dangerous out there?"

But Linus shook his head.

"We're walling ourselves off in here! There's a big, beautiful world just waiting to connect with us—like my new friends! They can't wait to meet everyone."

The citizens of Linneopolis
were skeptical at first.

Linus's new friends were certainly different.

But they soon discovered

"different" wasn't such
a bad thing.

And sometimes . . .

differences were truly
worth celebrating.

For DeAndré—
thank you for making
life so colorful

atheneum

ATHENEUM BOOKS FOR YOUNG READERS • An imprint of Simon & Schuster Children's Publishing Division • 1230 Avenue of the Americas, New York, New York 10020 • © 2023 by Stuart Hausmann • Book design by Rebecca Syracuse © 2023 by Simon & Schuster, Inc. • All rights reserved, including the right of reproduction in whole or in part in any form. • ATHENEUM BOOKS FOR YOUNG READERS is a registered trademark of Simon & Schuster, Inc. Atheneum logo is a trademark of Simon & Schuster, Inc. • For information about special discounts for bulk purchases, please contact Simon & Schuster Special Sales at 1-866-506-1949 or business@simonandschuster.com. • The Simon & Schuster Speakers Bureau can bring authors to your live event. For more information or to book an event, contact the Simon & Schuster Speakers Bureau at 1-866-248-3049 or visit our website at www.simonspeakers.com. • The text for this book was set in Futura LT Pro. • The illustrations for this book were rendered digitally. • Manufactured in China • 1022 SCP • First Edition • 10 9 8 7 6 5 4 3 2 1 • Library of Congress Cataloging-in-Publication Data • Names: Hausmann, Stuart, author, illustrator. • Title: Linus / Stuart Hausmann. • Description: First edition. | New York : Atheneum Books for Young Readers, [2023] | Audience: Ages 4-8. | Audience: Grades 2-3. | Summary: Sweet, plucky Linus cannot quite seem to fit into the rigid confines of his strait-laced world—and maybe that is not such a bad thing. • Identifiers: LCCN 2022009793 (print) | LCCN 2022009794 (ebook) | ISBN 9781665900300 (hardcover) | ISBN 9781665900317 (ebook) • Subjects: CYAC: Individuality–Fiction. | LCGFT: Picture books. • Classification: LCC PZ7.1.H38746 Li 2023 (print) | LCC PZ7.1.H38746 (ebook) | DDC [E]–dc23 • LC record available at https://lccn.loc.gov/2022009793 • LC ebook record available at https://lccn.loc.gov/2022009794